T0129930

Wing Over Wendover Meets the King

Eric Stephen Bocks

authorHOUSE®

AuthorHouse™
1663 Liberty Drive
Bloomington, IN 47403
www.authorhouse.com
Phone: 1 (800) 839-8640

© *2015 Eric Stephen Bocks. All rights reserved.*

No part of this book may be reproduced, stored in a retrieval system, or transmitted by any means without the written permission of the author.

Published by AuthorHouse   11/18/2015

ISBN: 978-1-5049-1041-5 (sc)
ISBN: 978-1-5049-1042-2 (e)

Library of Congress Control Number: 2015906861

Print information available on the last page.

Any people depicted in stock imagery provided by Thinkstock are models, and such images are being used for illustrative purposes only. Certain stock imagery © *Thinkstock.*

This book is printed on acid-free paper.

Because of the dynamic nature of the Internet, any web addresses or links contained in this book may have changed since publication and may no longer be valid. The views expressed in this work are solely those of the author and do not necessarily reflect the views of the publisher, and the publisher hereby disclaims any responsibility for them.

For
Ricky Ticky Tumble
Knows' a Rumble … Bera Bera Bisksy
National pom-pom!
And
The kid on the tricycle

CHAPTER 1

"A faire, a dream, and a girl"

TIMMY HAD BEEN ASKED to take Wendover, his prize peregrine falcon, to a Renaissance faire. His English teacher, Mrs. Tyler, had set up the day. He would have his own booth, dress in old English costume, and answer questions about falcons and falconry. Mrs. Tyler also told him to smile a lot as the people passed by.

He even had a pretty good little English accent too, because his sophomore class had just finished doing Shakespeare's comedy, *A Midsummer Night's Dream*. He had played the part of Nick Bottom, a would-be, could-be actor who gets a spell put upon him by Oberon, the fairy king, and is turned into a donkey. His "Hee haw, hee haw!" got a lot of chuckles from the crowd. He had rehearsed a lot with Sara, who played Tittania, queen of the fairies. Her character was also under a spell and was now "In Love" with him, or as reality would have it, with the donkey "hee haw!" Sara was a girl who was a friend, but he was working on combining those two words.

It was a warm day at the faire, and the BBQ meats, strong rich coffees, and Old World scents like patchouli filled the air. Wendover sat quietly on his perch, cocking his head from time to time. Every so often someone would come over and want to pet the bird or ask a question. A popular inquiry was, "How much does a bird like that cost?" Timmy always responded with "he's priceless."

The day was winding down, and Timmy was tired. He looked forward to flying Wendover. He hoped there would be some ducks on any of the ponds on his way home. He would like to see Wendover do his peregrine magic. On the drive back, he went from pond to pond, and spotted no wild game. It was going to get dark soon, but Timmy decided to try one more place.

The Bartlett ranch was a main staple on his list of hunting grounds; it was natural cattle land that had never been touched by human plow or chisel. Lots of ducks flew into the ponds on the property, and pheasant abounded. As he drove up to the gate, he met the caretaker, Dan. They shared some words and a warm handshake, and Timmy found out that Dan had just seen a couple of pheasant down the road around a berry patch. "If you get down there right now, I bet Wendover can catch dinner for ya!" Dan said.

Timmy rushed down the bumpy road to the berry patch. He secured the telemetry, turned on the receiver, and heard the old familiar *beep, beep, beep.* Then he struck

Wendover's hood, lifted him high over his head, and curled his gloved hand slightly as he let Wendover fly. "Now this is what I've been waiting for!" Wendover said to himself. The falcon wasted no time climbing up into the sky and shortly reached a good pitch. Timmy let Roxy, his pointing Lab, out of the truck and looked up to find Wendover straight up above him.

The falcon commanded the sky over the pheasant. He was up at about one thousand feet now and still climbing. Roxy locked onto the game bird. Her tail wagged twice as hard when she found a bird in the bush. Timmy waved his hat at Wendover as a signal to him to pay attention. Wendover looked down and waited for Timmy to flush. The hunting team was in place. "Go get' em Roxy!" Timmy kicked at the old rooster and Roxy pounced and the pheasant knew it was time to fly, and the bird exploded into the air and flew hard and fast for cover. There was another berry patch about three hundred yards away, and the bird arched in the air looking over his shoulder at the falcon and trying to get to the safety of the bush.

Timmy looked straight up and shouted, "Wing over, Wendover!" Then he watched as Wendover stooped down toward the pheasant. Timmy ran in the direction of the hunt, but something went wrong. He tripped and fell to the ground, bumping his head on a smooth but large rock. All the lights went out, and Timmy lay there unconscious with his falcon in the stoop on a collision course with the rooster pheasant.

When Timmy woke up, things were just as he had left them. Or were they …? He shook his head a little from the blow and wondered what had happened. He was not sure how long he had been out, but he looked into the sky and figured it had just been a blink as he caught a glimpse of Wendover as he finished his stoop and saw him hit the pheasant hard. The rooster cartwheeled over in a somersault and fell to the hard ground.

Timmy got up and felt the lump on his head. He was satisfied he was all right and started to walk toward the kill. It was then that he felt something strange by his side. He reached down, thinking it was a branch or weed he might have picked up from the fall. He tried to move it out of the way, but to his amazement he saw a broadsword in a scabbard. As he looked further down to his boots, he saw leather leggings. When he dusted off his shirt, he found the soft leather of a jerkin. Instead of his baseball cap, he had a hat with a silver pin holding a golden pheasant feather.

The next thing was the strangest indeed. He noticed two boys running and laughing about a hundred yards in front of him and they were headed for Wendover and the dead pheasant. He sprinted to save his bird. "Say there, what do you think you are doing? Get away from my prize bird!"

As the events unfolded, things got even weirder. Two men on horseback rode past Timmy towards the birds and boys. When he finally reached the group, panting and out of breath, Connie, the larger of the boys, turned and ran straight at him, tackling him to the ground. "*Your* prize bird?" The other boy picked up the falcon and then bowed quickly as the larger of the two men got off his horse. They all kneeled as the man moved slowly toward the falcon. Timmy was at first mesmerized by the scene. He stood looking as the man approached. The other boy, Stanley, pulled him down to kneel. Timmy dropped his head as if he had been bowing to kings all of his life.

The great man was dressed in a shirt made of cambric, and he had a leather jerkin made of light summer deer. He had a reddish beard, keen green eyes, and wore a crown. The older of the two men followed the crowned one and spoke in a smooth English accent. "Aye, my lord, Timothy has trained him well." The king peered at Wendover with intensity and obvious appreciation. He touched the small falcon with his finger, which sported a large ring with a blood stone and a family crest of a lion. He stroked the little bird's breast, and the falcon roused from the touch.

The boy who tackled Timmy piped up again. "He is the finest trainer of birds in the shire, even if he is me best mate."

"That'll be, Connie. Hold your tongue." The older man quipped. The king turned, looked at Timmy, smiled, nodded then mounted his horse and galloped off. The older man was a bit annoyed and looked at Connie. "I hope you boys haven't made the king angry with your foolishness. Tim, get yourself together and see to your bird. His Majesty will want a full recording of today's events. Tomorrow we host the king of France. Everything must be perfect. All the birds must be well tended to, sharp set, and ready to fly." Then the man looked at Wendover. "And you, my dear little tiercel, shall be a gift for the king of France."

Timmy frowned as Connie took the bird from Stanley and transferred it once more to him. "Sir, Wendover is to be given away?"

"You really did hit your head, didn't you, Son? Aye, you have been training this bird for just that end. Timmy looked into the man's clear blue eyes. "You're my Father aren't you," Timmy blinked. "Are you alright lad? Let's have a look at that bump." Cornelius rubbed Timmy's head around the wound. "Aye, you are my son, and I am proud of you, this is a good lump, but you'll be fine. Now, get some rest, and I'll see you back at the royal mews tout suite!"

Cornelius was indeed his father, he had taken the boy in at an early age and raised him as his own. He mounted his horse and rode off to meet the king. Timmy was in a daze all he could do was start walking slowly in the same direction. He looked on while the two other boys, Connie and Stanley, ran alongside his father's mare leaving him and Wendover at a snail's pace. Timmy looked at Wendover and saw that he was looking directly into his eyes. As Timmy met the bird's gaze, he heard a voice. "I do believe that the king was satisfied with my flight. Do you not think so?" Timmy looked around and for an instant, expecting to see Connie. "I say, Timmy, were you not pleased?"

Timmy looked at Wendover and thinking that he must be in some dream within a dream uttered. "Aye, little lad, you were stupendous." The moment the words left his mouth, he stopped, looked at Wendover, and rubbed the lump on his head. It *was* his voice, but he didn't normally talk like that. His thoughts were being translated into the King's English, and out the words shot as little English-accented arrows, as if he had spoken that way all of his life. He stared at Wendover in disbelief. He was positive he had never used the word "stupendous" before. Then it hit him: Wendover had never been in his head like this before either. No animal had.

"Are you all right?" asked Wendover. The bird's voice was clear and strong.

"I'm fine. I'm going bonkers, but I think I am just—"

Wendover cut in. "You're tired. You've sixteen falcons to get ready for tomorrow's hunt and only those two ninnies to help you." Timmy glanced over his shoulder at the two boys, who were now in a heap wrestling on the ground. "You'd better get us back to the royal mews."

Timmy took a long sigh and pondered this new twist that supposedly was his life. *Sixteen falcons to make ready to fly? I work for the king of England, I can hear Wendover when he talks to me, I have a father who loves me and two ninnies who are my best mates to help me get ready for the King of France... No problem here, eh?* Wherever he was and whatever dream this was, it felt real enough to let his doubts about all these things dissolve into the mist of the old

English countryside. He looked down again to the sword on his belt, and he grabbed the hilt and started to pull the sword from its scabbard but changed his mind. He touched the hat pin on his head with the pheasant feather, he looked at Wendover. "Aye, little man, we shall get back, but resting is not upon the list. We must get sixteen falcons ready to fly." Timmy walked with a confidence and anticipation of this new adventure, but there was a cloud over him, too. It hurt his heart when he remembered what Cornelius said about Wendover, and the words repeated in his head: *This bird is to be a gift to the king of France.* Timmy stopped and saw Wendover sitting like a little prince on his fist. "The king of France doesn't deserve you Wendover. We will have to see to this ..."

It was dusk when Timmy got back to the castle. He was amazed that he seemed to know just where to go, he'd forgotten the strange feeling he'd had after he hit his head. Now he was certain that everything was the way it should be. He walked through a barn-type enclosure as though he were royalty. There were guards posted outside with armor and long pikes. He saw Connie and Stanley in the corner cutting some leather as he entered the mews, he saw a huge perch thirty feet long with all sorts of different falconry birds upon it. Some birds were preening, some were sleeping, and some looked like they needed to be fed.

There was a place for Wendover, and Timmy put him up on the perch. His little bird fantastic roused, put his foot up, and watched his master. "I told you, did I not? Sixteen falcons to fly." Timmy looked down the line of birds. He walked slowly, inspecting each falcon, and he found he knew each by name. Then to his delight he remembered each bird's flying weight, what game they preferred, and what things scared them.

Then he saw "her." The Gyrfalcon. She was white as the English snow, pure and wild. She was the king's favorite. Her name was Lady Di. In those days it was decreed that kings were the only ones to keep and fly these magnificent birds, and Timmy knew why: they were hard to train, smart but stubborn. One moment they seemed to have the temperament of a child at play, but when they got serious, no other bird could match them in a tail chase. Lady Di was definitely a princess.

Connie broke Timmy's concentration when he tackled Stanley. "You see our lad Wendover today? He flew better than any bird the king has. The king is bloody bonkers to give him away." Connie had a deep cockney accent and spoke louder than most anybody. He had the heart of a saint, the mouth of a soldier, and the intelligence of a fox.

Stanley kicked him off and in the same accent coughed up a sentence to Timmy, still looking at the white gyr. "She's a beaut, ain't she? No other bird like her, one of a kind. Pity she won't take game yet."

Timmy had picked up the majestic bird and was stroking her. "She'll come through. She's got more royalty in her than any hundred falcons."

Connie burped and tugged at his jerkin. "Except for Wendover. He's the bloody Duke of York. And you, Timothy H. Barnes the first, master falconer and all around best mate, you are all stuck up and full of hot air."

Timmy secured Lady Di, snickered, and ran at the two boys, jumping a good three feet in the air. They all landed in a heap.

As the three wrestled, a mystery person snuck into the royal mews and watched the mayhem. Connie bit Stanley in the calf, and Stanley yelped. The three boys were covered in hay from top to bottom and were at a fever pitch, kicking, grabbing and laughing, trying to get the upper hand. Stanley now had Connie in a headlock, and Timmy was buried beneath them both. This was roughhousing at its best. As they were concentrating on the battle, the mischievous guest made her way to the water bucket. No one noticed, and she was able to position herself perfectly for the best results. She raised the bucket, counted under her breath to three, closed her eyes and threw the ice cold liquid as high as she could into the air. The boys screamed with shock and astonishment. They stood up, slipped again, and finally realized it was the maiden.

She was Timmy's fantasy. His heart did leap for purposes of romance, and as the boys composed themselves, they stood at attention in a straight line just right for any army inspection.

Sara walked slowly just as Timmy had done earlier, when he was evaluating his falcons. She picked a piece of hay out of Connie's mouth, and Stanley giggled as she quickly grabbed another from his hair, making him flinch. Then she reached Timmy and gave him a stern frown, looked him up and down ... and then burst into girlish laughter. "For boys in the service of the great King Richard of England on the eve of the most important day of your young falconry lives, I would say you should get cleaned up and ready for feast—and stop acting so foolish."

Connie and Stanley shrugged, looked at Timmy with a smirk, and ran off to change. Timmy stood calmly, covered from head to toe with wet hay. She turned to walk away and then looked over her shoulder. "Sir, you look like a scarecrow in the rain!"

Timmy spoke back in soft tones. "Alas, my lady, 'tis the appearance of a great hero that is often mistaken for a stuffed shirt. But if I am a scarecrow, then I should sow these wild oats with one far fairer and cleaner than I." He bent forward flourishing a large of a bow, lavishly using his arms and hands in precise motion. His head was tilted down toward his feet when with a burst of energy he surprised her by picking her up over his shoulder and dumping her into the soft wet hay.

She screamed. "How dare you! You are a rogue and a villain, and I should like to ... kiss you!" Time stood still. The long awaited moment of truth had arrived, and Timmy's dream was about to become real. He wasted no more time with words and kissed her tenderly upon the lips. The two lay in each other's arms for a moment, amazed at what had just happened. Sara smiled and wriggled free, and then ran off to get cleaned up for the upcoming feast. It was their first kiss, and although Timmy was wet and chilled from the water and itchy from the hay, he was the happiest lad in the world.

Wendover had watched the whole affair and added, "It's almost spring, my friend." Then he cleared his voice and looked at the

Boy who was in the daze from his first kiss. "The king of England awaits you, and if you are ever going to talk His Majesty out of making me a present to the king of France, you'd better get cleaned up."

Timmy looked at Wendover and smiled. "I will find a way, Wendover. You are my prize falcon." With that he ran to get cleaned up for the feast and to try to figure out how he would keep kissing the girl he loved—and save his favorite falcon from the clutches of the French king.

CHAPTER 2

"Ay tis me... and I shall vanquish all comers"

WENDOVER SAT WITH ONE foot tucked up against his body. He was the first in line on the long perch and watched the other birds stretch and sleep and do all the things birds of prey do when they are not hunting. He heard a rustle of dry straw and noticed a movement under the hay where the boys had been wrestling. It wiggled and vibrated as something underneath moved closer to the perch. It looked like a wave on a beach coming up to greet him. Finally at the end of the golden strands, there peeked out a little head, then a body. Then with far more fur than tail, there erupted a small pack rat. It was Diego Maximilian Jones, Wendover's trusted sidekick and very good friend. DJ, as the rat was known, carried a gold hat pin and waved it like a sword. He had just found it in the hay. The pack rat fought a mock attack, lunging and twirling, then with a squeak and a fine Irish brogue of an accent he said, "Aye, tis me… and I, and we doth challenge any and all that abound in this shire to raise their swords, and I shall vanquish all comers."

"That is Lady Sara's pin," Wendover announced.

The pack rat replied, "Aye, I know. I bring it to you even though this wee beauty would be a crowning piece in my family's ancestral treasure."

Wendover said, "You are a good friend."

Diego Maximilian Jones bowed his head, and smiled. "Any news upon the arrival of that skunk of a French king?"

A gyrfalcon three birds down added her thoughts to the conversation. And in a French accent noted "I was a gift from zi king of France to your king Richard and I think what you say about zi French king is not so nice. True, but not so nice." Izzy was a French gyrfalcon who never flew very high but was very aggressive on game. Her favorite thing to do was catch moor hen.

DJ started to laugh, and soon all the birds were in agreement. The consensus was that the French king's master falconer, Pierre la Dubois, drank too much wine and abused his birds. If they did not fly well, sometimes he would not feed a bird for days to get it to do what he wanted. More than once a bird had died in his care.

DJ started his questioning. "What is Timmy going to do? Can he save ya?"

Wendover was confident. "I flew for the king today, and after the flight he looked at me the way he looks at you, Lady Di. You know you are his favorite." He looked at the white gyr down the perch and she bowed her head ever so slightly as if taking court. "Timmy hit his head on a rock and acted very strange. He was not there to pick me up, and so Stanley got there first. Timmy has not been himself."

DJ hung his head, and a tear came to his eye; it fell as a perfect droplet upon the hay. "Timmy will never part from ya. You will see."

That night all the birds were fed and watered, primped and coddled, and allowed time by the fire. Everyone was fed the precise amount prescribed by Timmy. Connie had a fine tenor voice and sang to three of the king's favorite birds, who seemed to be nervous. The song was one King Richard the Lionheart had written himself.

Deep in the woods,
They say, they say,
Is Greenwood Glade, is Greenwood Glade,
Deep in the Sherwood Forest lay.
The deer do play; we bless this day
In Greenwood Glade

After the late-night workings, all the boys laid on their cots with heads upon pillows and dreams of making the next day perfect for the supreme royalty.

The sunrise with its shimmer of gold filled the huge old oak branches on the English countryside. The big day was thrust upon the bleary eyed lads. Yawns gave way to stretching and ice-cold water in the face. The hurried falconers worked hard in preparation for the day's big hunt. But alas, the king of France showed up too late to fly, and then he drank too much wine; the event was put off another day. The French entourage always seemed to have some excuse for not coming out of their tents.

Then as if scripted for a tragedy, the fog rolled in. Every promise of a flight with a falcon was broken. This gave Timmy some time to politic on Wendover's behalf and talk to his mentor and adopted father. The man's name was Cornelius of Orange, a title bestowed to him by the late King Henry II, King Richard's father. Cornelius had been made to choose sides in the royal politics of the day, and he had decided to support King Richard, praying he would take the crown. It was the right choice. Cornelius had been put in charge of the royal falcons when he was just sixteen years of age because of his understanding of birds of prey. King Harry, as he was called, had said to him, "Great falconers are born, not made," and Cornelius had proven the fact: he understood the way birds of prey thought. The King wanted his falcons to behave a certain way, and Cornelius bridged the gap between God anointed king, and bird. When Richard took the throne he would have no other person look after his royal mews.

Cornelius was teaching Timmy all his secrets, but Timmy was a born falconer, too, and had a fresh perspective and insight into each bird in his charge. Cornelius gave Timmy advice. "You see, lad, it is not enough just to have a falcon that flies high and takes game. The bird must be well mannered and respectful to anyone whom the king wishes." Cornelius and Timmy set the bar at the highest level possible. The king's falcons were spared no expense and were treated better than most humans of the day.

As soon as he could, Timmy got Cornelius aside to talk, and he brought up the "unmentionable subject" again. His father scoffed but listened with as much patience as he could muster. "Is there a chance the king might keep Wendover, my lord?" Timmy asked.

Cornelius sighed with frustration. He loved the boy as if he were his own. "We've been over this lad!"

Timmy broke in. "But after yesterday's stupendous flight, maybe he has changed his heart. You saw the way the king looked at Wendover. He actually got off his horse. He never does that for any bird unless it has surpassed his greatest of expectations."

Cornelius frowned, smiled, and frowned again. He knew the boy was right, but after all, Timmy was an emotional teenager and must be reminded that they were dealing with a king. "It is only on the good graces of the king that we have our livelihood, Tim. I would not presume to advise the king unless asked."

Timmy bit his lip. He knew there was no point in pleading. He used the only other tactic that made sense to him. He threw out his chest and said, "Then he shall see Wendover fly higher than he has ever flown. The king will be so impressed that he will not be parted from him. You will see. You will not have to say a word."

With that Timmy walked out of the mews—and bumped into Sara. She was holding the reins of a magnificent black stallion. She also carried with her the biggest smile. Timmy stopped, blushed, and then grinned. "Good morning, my lady." He moved around her, but she blocked his way, so he moved to the left. She countered, using the horse to block his getaway. "Sara, why will you not let me pass? I must run eight miles and hurry along a shipment of hawk food for the French king."

"Yes," she said. "But its closer to ten miles, and you must be back before it gets dark, or else the king of France will think the king of England is making an insult."

Timmy looked in her eyes. As frustrated as he was becoming, he would not raise his voice to her. "So… that's why I must go!"

She let him pass but turned and with a sing-song in her voice said with glee, "The King and I have a present for you."

Timmy turned, exhausted with this game playing. He quipped, "A present, for me? From the King … and you?"

"Well, I am the messenger, anyway. This magnificent beast is from King Richard. He said to say, and I quote, 'to that boy Tim that socked his head on that rock and flies the king's falcons." She lowered her voice an octave and gruffed out a man's voice. "Take this steed as a measure of my love and resolve that this horse may be more sure footed than he who rides it." She blushed, curtsied with a smile, and handed him the reins. Timmy's jaw dropped as Sara handed the horse over. "He rides well, too, with a wonderful gate. He walks smooth as your kiss."

Timmy felt the urge to take her in his arms and kiss her, but knew they were in public and that it was unthinkable.

He instead took her hand bent on one knee and kissed it. His new found steed took the opportunity to nozzle the lad and knock him off balance. Sara helped him up then the horse again pushed Timmy into Sara's arms. "Thank you, my lady. Since I will now be back early, having this trusty steed to shorten my trip, would you honor me with your company before the feast? In the presence of your mother, of course."

She smiled and repeated, "Of course."

Timmy climbed aboard the horse, touched him with his heels ever so slightly, and the animal responded with a power he had never felt. Timmy tried to sit straight in the saddle and act gallant and confident, just like a knight, but the stallion was testing his mettle with every moment. Poor Timmy was doing his best simply to stay in the saddle. He tried to end the conversation with decorum but his new horse turned to leave without his permission. "Then until later, my lady." His new mount galloped off with full measure, with Timmy holding on for dear life.

Back in the mews, Connie was holding Wendover, and Stanley was holding Lady Di. "She is without a doubt the most beautiful bird I have ever seen," stated Stanley.

Connie argued the point and proclaimed Wendover the supreme bird of the mews. The two started squabbling when Cornelius entered the mews. "Where is Tim?"

Connie shrugged, and Stanley shook his head "Dunno, my lord."

"You two make ready the birds. The king has called for the hunt. The French king is sober—at least right now—and has made a boast that his birds will outperform any English hawk in the field."

Connie asked, "How many birds to take, my lord?"

"All of them except that one." He pointed to Wendover. "No need to risk the gift. All right, get a move on—and find Tim!" The two put the birds away and started to make ready all the supplies for the hunt. Wendover looked down the perch at the massive white gyr. "You are without a doubt the most beautiful falcon I have ever seen," he said.

She cocked her head and spoke to Wendover. "Those are kind words coming from the king's most ruthless hunter."

Wendover roused and began preening. "I am Wing over Wendover, and I am going to be a gift to the king of France, but I would rather stay close to Timmy … and you."

The two were interrupted by the lads, who took up Lady Di and left Wendover on the perch. Connie shook his head. "I'm sorry, Wendover. This may have been the last chance you had to show the king you are the best bird he has ever seen fly. Where is Tim? He'd know what to do."

Timmy had not had the chance to tell anyone of the French king's request, and he knew that it would be an "issue politic" if both kings were to meet and the request was not filled. It was very bad indeed to not have exactly what a king wanted when he needed it. Timmy rode hard to the farm, where he was to pick up the basket of cockerels.

When he got to the home croft, the keeper had the birds ready; they were live, six-week-old chicks, and when Timmy checked the basket of what appeared to be a hundred or so little birds, they tried to jump for freedom. Timmy was too fast for the would-be escapees and returned the heavy cloth that topped the basket just in time.

"These are wild ones," the keeper said slowly, "but they is fit for any Frenchie king's bird, I'll guess."

Timmy took a step toward the man and looked him down. "They'd better be healthy, or it will be both our heads."

The old man cackled and coughed. "Oh, they is, they is!"

Timmy climbed back on the horse, and the keeper handed him the basket. Timmy looked his new stallion in the eye and stroked the creature. "A mammoth like you must have a name, and since you're mine I will christen thee ..." He thought for a moment "Farvel. Fit for a king, but just right for His Majesty's master falconer." Farvel reared up to a stance, and Timmy knew the name was true. "Whoa, I've got to get these chicks to King Phillip, or there will be the devil's own to pay."

Timmy started off and at first moved slowly. Sara was right about Farvel: he had a wonderful gate that was smooth and strong, and his temperament was balanced and calm. The small expedition started off upon the king's road. Timmy started to whistle a tune and daydream. He let his mind wander, thinking about Sara, her smile filled his heart. He thought of their first kiss, closed his eyes when all came to catastrophe. Three French riders in a dead run and swearing at him in French rode past him, spooking Farvel to such a pitch that it was clear something bad was about to happen. Up went Farvel, and as he reared back in his fullest majesty, down went Timmy not so gloriously, toppling over the basket to the hard ground and almost landing on his sword. He ended up sitting in the dirt with the basket upon his head and a mouth full of feathers. Little chicks ran in every direction. Timmy composed himself as best he could and started to try to catch the mass of escapees.

Then more chaos filled the air. A horn sounded *ta, taa ta, taa.* Timmy looked down the road to see horses and soldiers, the dust now added to the annoyance of trying to find the chicks. Just when he thought he would give up, he saw a king. It was *his* king, and he rode aside the French king. "Kings, kings, kings," he muttered under his breath as the procession came to a dead stop.

A single man started to announce the long presenting of the titles. "Oh hear ye, oh hear ye, comes lord. The king of all England and Ireland …" As the trail of verbiage slung across the forest green, yellow chicks ran here and there.

King Richard abruptly put a stop to the speech. "You there, boy."

Timmy bent his neck toward the booming voice, and with the sun in his eyes, he grasped four or five cockerels in his hands. As his eyes met the king's gaze, he saw a glimmer of a smile. "Tis Tim, my liege. I am master falconer to …"

"I know who you are, little stump. Why is my favorite master falconer steeped in small chickens?"

Timmy walked to the basket, now filled with three-quarters of the flock, and placed the handful of chicks into it. He covered it and stood as tall as the situation would allow. "The most treasured and most excellent king of France requested supplement for his fine hawks."

King Phillip nodded. "Oui, Your Majesty."

Timmy continued. "I was pursuing this very deed when my horse—the very steed that you hath given to me—was abruptly startled by the king of France's entourage. My horsemanship, not being what it should be, I fell to the ground, and the basket of royal cockerels were freed to be on some hungry fox menu. I have three-quarters of the cost retained and was in pursuit of the rest." There was a long silence and Timmy began to sweat. Connie perspired uncontrollably, and Stanley and Cornelius were so nervous that they felt sick.

"Ha!" was the response from Richard. The crowd looked at the English king. The French king giggled, and the two then opened up their hearts to full-blown hilarity. The crowd chimed in on cue. "My dear lad Tim, you have done your king and country well. We will wait for you. The hunt would not be the same without the presence of such a valued falconer. But my dear boy, have you lost my gift? Where is your steed?"

Just then Timmy saw that Sara had snuck her way to see the hunt and now walked through the crowd with the black beauty. She handed the reins to Timmy, who stood silent and somewhat dumbfounded. "Here, my lord," Timmy said with a blush. The king smiled as he looked at the two smitten teenagers and the love of spring in their midst. Timmy added "I have named him Farvel, and he is as magnificent as your prize falcon, Wendover."

Cornelius intervened as Timmy bowed. "Tim meant your falcon Lady Di, my liege."

The king smiled again and exclaimed, "All who would follow a king, to a hunt… to the hunt!" Oh, and Master Tim, I will look forward to seeing Wendover fly on this fine day of hawking."

The horns blew again and the party was off. Cornelius hung back and said "Well, that's rich, Tim. Now you must go back and retrieve your special Wendover. Meet us at the second clearing. We will set camp and hope the French king does not drink too much whilst we wait on you."

Timmy answered back seriously and confidently, "Start with one of Phillip's falcons. He will surely fly off. By the time it is back on the fist, Wendover will be in the sky."

Cornelius frowned, smiled, and then frowned once more. "So be it, then."

CHAPTER 3

"I love that Boy"

DJ WAS VERY CONCERNED about his friend. Questions flew out of the pack rat's little brain frantically. "So what is going to happen Wendover? Is the king going to give ya away? All the birds are talking about it. Do ya want to go? Or would ya rather stay? What happens if …?"

Wendover shook his head. "Diego Maximilian Jones, please stop! Timmy will have to do what the king commands. My fate is not mine to decide. I am a falconry bird, trained to fly for a king. I will do my duty …" He hung his head, sorrow filled his heart, and he breathed a heavy sigh. "I would miss the boy who trained me. We have a special bond and understand each other." Then he raised his chin and with a half cock of his head said, "I love that boy." DJ's tears flowed, and he rubbed his eyes.

Just then a storm erupted into the mews. It was not a grand entrance. Timmy flew in on Farvel with dust and dirt flying everywhere. Wendover was taken by surprise.

DJ was almost trampled. Timmy jumped off the steed and ran to Wendover with a huge smile on his face. "We have another chance, Wendover! The king wants to see you fly."

Wendover looked at Timmy. "Then we will give them the spectacle of a lifetime."

"They wait for us in a clearing across from Sherwood Forest, at the estate of the Earl of Loxley's." Timmy picked up Wendover, hooded him, and mounted Farvel. DJ, seeing his chance to join the team took a running leap and with the skill of an acrobatic hurled himself into Timmy's saddle bag that just so happened to contain a morsel of soft bread and a nut. "Mmm, lunch." Then the team was off. Timmy rode the big black stallion through camp as if he were a knight. The falcon on his fist sat like a little prince, and everyone who saw them whispered that this day was going to be special. Timmy, the youngest master falconer ever in the shire, would do proud their king and country. The king might even pronounce a day in his honor and a feast for all.

It took a good two hours to make the trip back to the king's hunting party. As Timmy returned to the scene where he had lost the chickens, one lone little cockerel wandered into the road. Timmy pulled his horse back to a stop. He looked down at the little chick and suddenly had a pang of compassion in his heart. It was defenseless, walking food for King Phillip of France, but something in Timmy wanted to save it. He needed to save this bird. He got off his horse, ran down the bird, and scooped it up. The tiny eyes glistened in the sun. "You, my dear illustrious chicken, are pardoned in the name of King Richard of England." He used his index finger as a sword in his mock ceremony and dubbed it shoulder to shoulder. "There, all is done." He climbed back on his horse and rode on to find the royal hunting party.

It was not long before he came to the crowd. A little lass of six years old sat on her father's lap, waiting as everyone was for the next event. Timmy got off Farvel, walked to her, and poured the little bird into her small hands. She smiled, and he saw that her two front teeth were missing. "For you, my lady, May this chick be healthy and strong and lay many eggs for your family." Her father looked at him in disbelief but then smiled and nodded in appreciation for the gift.

Timmy moved with purpose to the king's corner of the camp and saw the sight he held above any other. Fifteen falcons in various moods and positions waited for his direction. He placed Wendover in his spot and barked orders to Connie, who was flirting with one of the French king's entourage. "Connie, get Lady Di ready." Connie saluted to the now very serious, boss-like falconer, and soon Timmy held Lady Di on his fist. He called the king's dog keeper and asked for Bella, a blue Belton English setter of two years old. She was young and green in experience but had stamina and a fine nose. Cornelius joined the group and saw that Timmy looked weathered and worn but was happy to be there.

Timmy and Connie held Bella and bowed to the kings. The French king whispered in his broken English accent to Richard as he threw down another grog of ale. "And what do we have here? Zi lady with zi most perfect smile, zi white gyr I have heard so much about."

Cornelius bowed and cleared his voice. "Yes, sire. She is like no other, but she is just in her first year my liege and knows little. She is still playful with prey rather than exacting in her desire to kill."

Timmy cut in. "Yes, she is beautiful, my lord, and oftentimes playful, but today will be her first kill, and it will be in your honor. I can feel it!"

King Richard saw through the ruse but decided to play along. Richard shouted to let the dog run, and the group moved on as the dog put her nose to the air, then to the ground; she repeated the action in matching cadence to the breeze, which was faint but constant. She was searching for a point on a pheasant. The group walked only a hundred yards into the clearing when Bella locked on to a scent. Connie moved closer and in a soft whisper told the dog, "Whoa, hold 'em there, Bella." The two kings walked close to the point, and Timmy brought Lady Di to King Richard. Another attendant brought the royal gauntlet and held it up high. The king filled it with his massive hand, which was more used to slinging a sword or mace. As the fingers reached full extension in the soft deer leather, the king turned slightly, and Timmy was spot on with the falcon and transferred the bird. Connie saw Bella start to break. "Whoa back, Whoa back!"

Tension was becoming high, but the king would not be rushed and was not through admiring the falcon. "They say you are fast, young Lady Di. Show us your speed and take this prey with firm commitment, and yes, do it for my brother, the king of France."

Richard nodded to Tim, who looked around the brambles here and there until he saw the color of the pheasant. The red around the eyes and the green of the head shone through like Christmas morning. Timmy looked back at the king and said, "At your pleasure, my liege."

Richard smiled, removed the falcon's jesses, and then removed the hood. Lady Di roused seemingly without a care in the world. Connie was still praying the dog would hold the set, and she did. Richard inched forward. "Ho, Ho Ho!" the king yelled. Timmy kicked the bushes, Bella pounced and flushed the pheasant, and the game bird blasted off with the ancient scream of his ancestors. Lady Di flinched but focused intently on the would-be escapee as the game bird flew away. The king expected her to fly right off his fist and make a quick end to the prey, but she held to his glove, fast gripping down upon it. The party watched with disbelief as the falcon cocked her head first to one side and then the other, then almost all around and upside down as the pheasant flew from her, now about seventy-five yards away. The king looked at Timmy and frowned a bit.

Timmy said, "Aye, my king. Tell her to fly. Allez!"

Richard looked to the gyr, and just as the king made a sound, she pushed off his glove with all her might.

It would be a tail chase fit for kings. Connie started running after the pair. Both kings mounted their steeds with vigor. Cornelius rode in back, and the three took off, watching the falcon in its headlong chase. Timmy stood and watched the flight from where he had started. Lady Di flew hard in pursuit of the pheasant and was gaining on the bird but was still a hundred yards away. The pheasant had time in his favor; the brambles, his only safety from sure death, were not fifty feet away. However, the falcon turned on her miraculous speed. King Richard halted the group to watch her close in. It was like the pheasant was caught in slow motion. Lady Di made up the distance in a heartbeat and reached the prey. With one last strong flap of her wings, she inverted herself, going underneath to grab the bird and took it to the ground. Cheers and jeers commenced as the English yelled "Huzzah! Huzzah!" But the French entourage glanced from side to side in jealousy. When the king got to the sight, he saw the two birds fighting on the ground. The falcon was the bigger of the two, but none the less it was a mighty battle. Timmy and Connie finally caught up to the show. Timmy made in on the falcon gently who by now had dispatched the pheasant. He got down on his knees and reinserted her jesses and then her leash. He picked her up on the leg of the pheasant and handed her off to her king.

King Richard beamed like he had won a war, and Phillip moved closer to see the bird. "Magnifique, beautiful. She is a jewel." Timmy, Connie, and Cornelius bowed in concert to the praise. King Richard looked at the French monarch's adulation of the white bird and spoke to the French king's master falconer, who looked to be rather drunk and sneered at the whole affair. "Master falconer Dubois, my good brother King Phillip has boasted to me of a bird in your mews of such magnificence. Surely you cannot keep it in its hood all day. Prithee, let your falcon do its great king and my good brother the honor of the next flight. Loose the bird on the prey of your choice."

Pierre la Dubois bowed and then raised his head, revealing his missing teeth. "By your king's leave, I will fetch the bird. But may I request we move further on to the marshes, my lord? This falcon should like to kill a great blue heron."

Richard boomed back. "I must ask you, do you have the power to talk to your falcons and do they understand you?" Dubois stood as if he were frozen on a stage and had forgot his lines. "It is said my master falconer Tim knows what his birds are thinking." Before Pierre could respond, the King added in loud celebration made a toast, "Pray tell, to all who have ears to listen, to Tim and his talent. He hath honored us with a fine flight."

The crowd yelled, "Huzzah, huzzah to Tim!"

Pierre slowly moved off as the applause swelled. He was in a jealous, smoldering rage as the group reveled in Timmy's celebrity. Cornelius, Connie, and Stanley beamed as Timmy acted his humble self. The group disbursed and went off to pack up for the next ride to the marsh.

Sara brought Farvel to her sweetheart; she blushed and was so proud. He looked at her, and her hair seemed to glow in the sun. It looked to Timmy like there were beams of light coming out of her eyes and fingers. She spoke, "Congratulations on a wonderful flight."

Connie was nearby, and he parroted the words and tried to make them sound silly. "Congratulations on a wonderful—"

Sara frowned at Connie, and about the same time Stanley came in and tackled the boy. "Leave 'em to it, Connie!" Stanley yelled as the boys went to the ground. Sara walked Farvel, Timmy smiled and Sara beamed. Then the young lad made his big move and offered her his hand, palm down. She put her hand on his, and they strolled back to camp.

Pierre la Dubois had been born into a family of master falconers to the king of France. His grandfather's father's father had been one of the youngest ever to be given the post. Pierre la Dubois was not going to be outdone by an impertinent lad of English blood. One way or another, he would exact his revenge upon this boy falconer. He knew just how to do it; he had lots of practice in his younger days upsetting flights of other nobles when his father's job was on the line. The king of France would gamble on the success of the flights, and he did not like to lose. Pierre thought to himself, *I will distract the bird with a lure when it is the sky, so that it comes down to nothing. Or I'll loose a goshawk from the woods to fight with the king's falcon. There are ways to fix that boy.*

Soon the large hunting party moved north to the wetlands and marshes. The sun was starting to wane, but with luck, Dubois had scouted a great blue heron. The massive bird stood in the center of a small outlet hunting crayfish. The kings rode within one hundred yards of the bird, and Dubois waited on ceremony as the French king was helped off his horse. Protocol was much the same as the first flight. Phillip stuck his hand in the air and had a glove snugly attached. Then the king was brought the bird. She was also a gyr falcon, but she had not molted well and showed signs of year-old feathers that did not match the new ones. Dubois stepped up and cleared the way for the king, pushing down tall weeds. The dogs that the king of France hunted were Wolfhounds, and the three were brought out and held at bay.

When the king was ready, he shouted, "Allez! Allez!" The huge dogs were released and moved quickly, splattering mud and water in their wake. The heron squawked and took off in fight. The king of France did not like to strike the braces of the hood because of a childhood mishap where a falcon had bitten him on the lip, so Dubois raced to his side and slid the hood off the bird, trying hard not to obscure the falcon's line of sight. King Richard smiled, looked at Tim, and pursed out his lower lip in mockery of the French king.

Off went the falcon after the heron, and it was spectacular. Everyone viewed the majesty of the heron's 6 foot wingspan and its remarkable speed. The falcon curved under and over the massive bird, trying to force it down. Finally the heron had enough and started to climb. It looked for a moment that the falcon was going to be beaten, but she gave a burst of energy and flew almost straight up and twenty feet over the heron. Then she stooped down and grabbed the heron's head in her talons, and the two somersaulted to the earth for a battle on the ground.

Again the two kings rode, and the falconers ran to the prize. However, when they got to the scene, the sight was grim. The dangers in the art of falconry are many, but this was the risk that Dubois took when he chose the quarry. The falcon lay dead on the ground; it had been impaled by the Herons sharp beak. The king was furious, and he reined his horse hard and galloped off toward camp.

King Richard got off his horse and stood beside the two birds. He looked at the heron, blood trickled down its large thin beak. "You have won the war, my friend," he spoke in calm tones to the heron, who was now trying to poke the king's boot with its sharp beak. The King picked up the limp body of the falcon. "Noble, too, are you." Timmy took the bird from his hands and passed the creature on to Dubois's attendant, Oscar, who had tears in his eyes. Timmy felt sorry for the lad, who was not much older than him. He thought of Wendover and how lucky he had been. The hunting for the day was over, and Pierre la Dubois was nowhere to be seen.

CHAPTER 4

"Make this so, or you may well lose more than your job"

A LARGE CAMP HAD BEEN set, and the feast was being prepared. The tents of the kings stood at opposite sides of the camp. The colored banners of the monarch's hung high in the air. A great fire was lit in the center of the encampment, and guards from both countries lined the perimeter inside and outside. Small tents were pitched outside the camp by onlookers. Music could be heard from inside the kings' tents. Timmy, Connie, and Stanley stayed in the royal mews, and were busy seeing to all the raptors' needs.

Meanwhile, in King Phillip's tent, Dubois apologized for the day's event. "My liege, please forgive an old falconer his unfortunate fate."

Phillip chided the master. "Let one mistake be just that, Dubois. Two faux pas may well mean your position. Let tomorrow be that of glory. Fly the black jerkin and let the stage be set for success."

Dubois bowed and smiled with that grin missing two teeth from obvious neglect. "Of course, my king. All will be set for the benefit of gambling when the birds are set to fly."

"So it seems we understand the plan. Make this so, or you may well lose more than your job."

Dubois's eyes widened as he bowed again and left the tent with a flourish. Once outside he scratched his head, looked in vain for Oscar, and yelled to his attendant. "Oscar!"

Timmy and Sara had found their way to the feast, and they sat at the far right of the king. The king piped up loudly with an announcement, "Let it be said that true love is in our midst!" Timmy wanted to disappear with embarrassment, but he knew once the king had taken up a subject, he would not let it go.

"Love, my friends, is like war, and, it is the battle of every man to love a woman with honor and all his heart." Then he looked directly at Tim. "My dear Tim, I will state this honestly not just because I am king and my word is the law of the land, but because it is true ..." He held up his golden chalice filled with ale and toasted. "Tim loves Sara, and Sara doth love Tim, and this fine union we doth sanction in our hearts." He looked at the two and saw their smiles. Then he reached for his lute, which Cornelius had pulled from out of nowhere. The instrument was customarily nearby all the king's dinner tables. The king burst out in song.

To love the beauty of a flower,
All life's pleasure, its fine sweet smell.
For there shall be no other,
For Sara to Tim, and Tim to Sara,
And only the king can tell.

The table laughed and cried out, "Huzzah!" Tim and Sara held hands. The king continued with his lively banter and spoke to Cornelius. "A falcon's life is to kill or be killed, just like a king. Let today be a reminder to all that life is fleeting."

Cornelius raised his wine and spoke. "To the king. Long live King Richard of England!"

Timmy broke in just before the applause. "And to Wendover, the king's prize falcon!" Tim stood up and dropped his voice to a soft and serious tone. "And may tomorrow bring a flight worthy of Our Majesty." Again the party erupted into more merriment.

All cheered but Dubois. He clapped with only two fingers upon his palm, a tentative resolve. The king of France nodded to Dubois and they both smiled evilly. Timmy saw it, and so did Cornelius, who hoped their king had seen the unhealthy display.

The group ate venison and drank wine. The pheasant Lady Di had caught had been smoked, and it was tender meat that the king's enjoyed. When all were full in their bellies, the feast was declared over by the kings, and they made their way to their separate sides of the camp. Snoring of the great ones was soon followed by dreams of the hunt.

Back in his tent, Pierre la Dubois was busy plotting. He had to have a plan, and an even darker backup plan, He had never seen Wendover fly. This bird could make a fool of him and maybe even create a circumstance where he could lose his job—or worse yet, his head. Oscar sat on a stool listening to his rants.

"Oscar, take two men and trap several pheasant. Also, see if you can find a young sparrow hawk, one that cannot fly well. Maybe a brancher. We will need twine and a cage with sharp sticks, maybe a hundred affixed to the cage and sticking straight up into the air."

Oscar frowned as he heard the plans. He loved falcons and did not like seeing any raptor hurt. But Dubois was his master, and he knew the king of France all too well.

"Oh, and one more thing. Find me a goshawk. Buy it and make sure it is sharp enough to attack anything."

It was well-known that King Phillip drank wine, and when he drank, he liked to gamble. When he gambled, he did not like losing, especially to the king of England. On hunting trips Phillip would bet on anything, the height of the birds, the method of the kill, or even whether the bird would grab onto the prey or hit it out of the sky. King Richard played the game but preferred not to gamble on his falcons. Phillip would throw fits of anger, and Richard would give in to the proceedings.

Oscar and his helpers got to work and spent the rest of the night trapping wild pheasants and building the cage of death.

The next morning Oscar went into town and enquired around and found a boy who kept a winning goshawk. He paid the boy a small fortune for the bird and told him to keep quiet about the transaction. But as Oscar left the boy's home, his father saw the French king's runner and saw that he was taking away the bird. He shouted at the man, but Oscar and the two riders rode away. He ran to find his son and asked him what had happened.

"Well," said the fourteen-year-old, "this man came and offered me three pieces of gold for old Aggie. I was going to give you the gold, Father, I promise I was."

"All right, lad, you're not in trouble. But why would the French king pay for a bird he does not even fly?" The two looked down at the gold in the boy's hand and pondered the question.

The morning was cold and overcast. Fires were built extra-large in camp to keep everyone warm, and the king was up early inspecting his army of falcons. He found Timmy taking care of a first-year falcon that had contracted an ailment called bumble foot. Timmy took turns cleaning the foot and wrapping it with salve comprised of seaweed ash and eucalyptus oil. The king smiled as he saw his young master falconer hard at work. "You do your family proud, young lad."

Timmy bowed and looked at the king. "You are my only family, my lord. That is to say, you and the falcons." Then a faint memory crossed his mind. He saw a woman in her thirties. His sister, maybe?

The King sparked conversation. "What of your family?"

Timmy put his hand up to his head and scratched at his scalp. "Your Majesty, I do not remember them. But sometimes I get little pieces of the world I knew before. I do remember a woman. Every time I think of her, I feel warm in my heart. Alas, the memory is fleeting, and tis gone." The bird he was tending to cocked her head as if to say thanks.

The king saw again the special connection Timmy had with birds of prey. Richard looked at Wendover. The bird was handsome, there was no doubt of that. His cere was as yellow as primroses and the same vibrant color matched his feet. His eyes were bright and at ease at the same time. He looked at the king with a knowing confidence that only few falcons in a thousand show to their masters.

"This Wendover ... You think very highly of this bird, do you not?" the king asked.

"Yes, my lord. I love him. He is the most valuable bird in your mews."

"But he is just a peregrine. Surely Lady Di matches his swiftness and cunning. Gyrfalcons are for kings, are they not?"

Timmy bowed his head in protocol and answered the king in wise tones that made him sound older than his sixteen years. "My lord king, I have seen Wendover fly higher and faster than any in your mews. But his biggest strength is not speed or agility. It is in the mind of the bird that sets him apart. His confidence, and instinct alone, cannot be taken for granted. But in short, my king, his most valuable asset is that he <u>thinks</u> better than any other bird I have flown. In this he is very much like you, my liege."

The king listened to the speech and smiled. "Well then, he will make the finest of gifts to the king of France." Richard looked at Tim and saw his disappointment and his tone deepened. "You see, Tim, after years of petty squabbles and fighting I wish peace with King Phillip. If this extraordinary falcon can bring us closer to that end, then it shall be the most honorable use of this bird: to save lives." Timmy bowed, the king put his large hand on Tim's shoulder. "But alas, worry not my young master. You hath honored the king with your talents, and your insight and love of birds of prey hath made my heart glow. You will be rewarded, you will see. Make ready the wonderful Wendover. He will fly last today, and then we will make him a gift of peace." Richard left the mews in great stride.

Tim thought long and hard about what the king said, and he tried in his heart to let Wendover go. "Peace," he whispered to himself. He stared at him and spoke. "Today you fly for all of England, Wendover. I have no doubt our last flight together shall be perfect and true. The king has honored you as a gift of peace, and we shall not let him down."

Wendover roused and spoke inside Timmy's head. "For king, for country … and for YOU!"

Timmy could not contain his feelings. He had to tell someone of his revelation, so he went to find Cornelius. He was at the entrance of camp seeing to the hunting expedition's needs. Timmy came up behind him while Cornelius was busy ordering men about, "No, you idiot, over there." He almost hit Timmy in the mouth with his finger. Timmy ducked, and Cornelius chattered on. "So you think you can sneak up on an old man, eh?" He smiled, "what can I do for you lad?"

"Would you walk with me, my lord?" The two started to stroll in the direction of the royal mews. Father tried to size the son up, but Timmy saved his lord the trouble of having to pry it out of him. "My lord, the king has decreed that for the purposes of peace, Wendover shall be his finest gift to the king of France. Furthermore, it is for this cause that he gives away his finest bird. My lord, nothing must stand in the way of a fantastic flight today. But I fear Dubois has plans to topple the friendship of the kings."

"Young Tim, you are wise for your age, and you have fine instincts, but this game you speak of is best played by older, wiser, men like me." Cornelius revealed his contagious smile and winked at Timmy. "You leave the dirty work to the ones that know it. Fly high your Wendover, and let me worry about the dark side of Pierre la Dubois and the king of France"

Timmy blurted out, "Don't forget Oscar. I don't trust that boy."

Cornelius winked. "I won't forget Oscar." He went back to commanding his men before stopping short and looking at Tim. "Tim, did you know that Oscar lived in England for a time? He trained with me. Then his mother was called to King Phillip's court."

Timmy frowned and sighed. "You are right, Father. I will let you handle the intrigue. I'll stick to flying falcons." They hugged and went separate directions.

Timmy was in search of Connie when he saw Sara. She was walking out toward the camp's north exit. He called to her, but she didn't hear him, so he followed her. She was walking quickly and was always just out of reach, Timmy quickened his pace to a jog. Finally after passing through the northern gate, she disappeared. He stopped and felt torn. He thought he should go after her, but time was short and he had to see to all the birds. He made the bold choice and ventured down the path he thought she had taken.

After some brambles and fallen logs, he came upon a small clearing, and he saw her. The sun seem to break through as she entered the glade. He was just about to call out to her name when something unexpected happened. She looked toward the thick forest and reached out her arms and who should appear to fill them but Oscar? Timmy ducked down behind the berry bush and watched as they hugged and carried on. Sara kissed Oscar on his cheek. Timmy could not believe it as they hugged again, this time for a long time. They had a quick dialogue, and then she turned to return the way she had come.

Timmy ran like the wind, there was a storm in his heart. He held back the tears and his anger. He made it back to the mews huffing and puffing. One of the guards asked him if something was wrong, and Timmy made an excuse. His heart had just been broken and he was not sure what to do. Moments before he had promised Cornelius that he would let him handle the intrigue, but that was before Sara was involved. He thought, *Sara, what are you thinking, aiding the king of France's twisted affairs? With Oscar? You even kissed him! I thought you loved me.*

Connie saw Timmy and tried to tackle him into the hay, but Timmy evaded the attempt and pushed him aside like a professional soldier, where he narrowly missed a plough. "Hey, what's with you?" Connie said at the close call.

"Not now, Connie. We've got falcons to get ready to fly." Then Timmy did something he had never done before: he yelled at Connie. "Get on with it!" He left the mew, leaving Connie hurt and shaking his head.

The royal hunting party was soon on the road again, and the kings decreed that they would fly as many falcons as they could while the weather was good. In King Richard's heart was his promise of peace. In Phillip's head was a passion for gambling and to best the great Richard the Lionheart at any cost.

Timmy rode Farvel, and he was getting worried. He had a little time to think about everything, and now he was having concerns about Sara's safety. Cornelius rode aside the king like the wise old man he was, answering questions about this and that. Dubois rode just behind his King and was thinking of his terrible plan fixed down to every awful detail. He was confident that at the end of the day, his king would be victorious, the great Wendover would be dead, and he would still have his job. Oscar rode behind him with his henchmen to help carry out the plan.

At long last a site was chosen for the next hunt, and Timmy was summoned off the line and was told to fly Bessie, one of the king's favorites. She was a six-year-old peregrine and had killed many game birds. The king thought he should like to see her on water fowl of some sort. Timmy took up the bird and the smaller hunting party consisting of the kings and their master falconers walked out into the open marsh. Richard took a deep breath of the fresh clean air and exhaled. "I do believe that I would just as soon be hawking than fighting a battle."

The French king laughed and snidely commented, "Oh Richard, you have never been so happy than when you are laying siege to one of my castles. You must admit it."

The red-haired king smiled and looked into Phillip's eyes. Then he moved in so close he could smell the wine on the French king's breath. "My brother king, I wish peace above all other things."

Phillip retorted, "Then give back the Aquitaine, and we shall be friends forever."

Richard laughed out loud, and the booming roar of the Lionheart flushed some of the mallards on the creek. He laughed again to see the hunt once again being ruined by politics. "Let us hunt, instead of talk of lands and crowns and barons and clowns."

Phillip spit downwind and sneered. "Oui, let us fly this slip. I will wager you ten gold pieces that the bird binds to the duck instead of hitting it out of the sky, and another twenty that your bird misses it because she is not paying attention."

Timmy was holding Bessie and bit his lip. He wanted to chime in and tell the king that Bessie was as solid as a flying rock and would not falter. Richard agreed to the bet, and the bird was let loose to fly. Connie and Stanley had the ducks picked out and were ready to flush. Bella was held on leash and was ready to run. Oscar had gone missing, and Timmy scanned the field to see if he could see any sign of him. Dubois stood next to the French king and smiled at Timmy. Bessie rung up in powerful wing strokes to a fast three hundred feet, and the ducks on the creek were getting nervous at seeing the predator in the sky. They fretted as they swam from bank to bank. This was where Timmy had learned to be patient and wait, Bessie climbed higher into the sky and went wide flying away from the creek and what seemed to be a clean catch. Dubois looked at Phillip and smiled again, thinking the flight was now ruined by an out of position falcon. "What do you say Richard double or nothing?" The Lion heart looked at Timmy winked and agreed to the bet.

Timmy whistled, and the bird started to return. She was now at one thousand feet and smack dab over the creek commanding the air space. Timmy looked at the king and spoke. "By your leave, Your Majesty."

The king smiled at the lad and snickered at the French monarch then yelled at the top of his lungs, "Ho! Ho! Ho!" Connie let loose Bella, and Stanley whooped and hollered. The ducks exploded off the creek. Bessie saw her charge and stooped. Her dark silhouette against the sky and looking like a teardrop, she whacked the duck out of the sky then came down in a flutter. She landed on the bird and started to pluck the fowl. Phillip scoffed, and Dubois looked away as Richard smiled from ear to ear and said, "It is a fine day." The falcon and its prey were displayed before the Kings and the group reveled in its success, wine was poured and ale drunk "Let the king of France be next. And Phillip, I will not bet on this next flight. We shall enjoy the frame with no distractions of the gold I may win." Phillip huffed but relented and ordered Dubois to task.

He found his prize bird, an old black Gyrfalcon of ten years. The bird had the heart of a hunter and the stamina of a horse. Phillip announced as he saw the bird, "We shall ride and flush the first prey that comes up, and this bird shall do us proud…Magnifique!" Richard and Phillip mounted, as did Oscar.

Dubois looked at Timmy and sneered. "No need for you to come, little lad. We can handle this just fine."

Timmy looked for King Richard's ruling on the issue. Richard issued his majestic response, "Master Tim shall ride with us all, as he is still young, Monsieur Dubois, and

I am sure he can learn many techniques from such a wise old falconer."

The party looked at Dubois, who slowly smiled, showing his lack of teeth. "Of course my liege. Whatever the king wishes."

Richard shot back, "I *do* wish it."

They started the ride with Dubois in front holding the falcon, followed by the two kings. Next were Oscar and Timmy. Cornelius dismissed himself because he had to use the privies. As they rode, the kings' dogs once again coursed the field, sniffing and searching out something to fly.

Timmy looked at Oscar and whispered, "I do not know what you are up to, but you won't get away with it."

Oscar was caught off guard, and he winced a little as his horse hit a bump. "What is it that I am up to, pray tell?"

Timmy was caught in his words, which he could not back up. He looked at Oscar and said, "I'll be watching you."

The pace quickened, and the dogs seemed to be on something. They rushed through the marshes. Dubois yelled, "Get ready," and he pulled the hood off the falcon. What happened next was filled with thunderous confusion. The dogs sprang up and down, and out came wild boar. Dubois released the falcon early, thinking it was to be some kind of a bird. The bird flew for the wild hog and knocked it on the head. King Richard started to laugh and quipped, "We shall have pig for supper, caught by a falcon!" It was then that the rest of the pack of pigs decided to break. They were everywhere and totaled forty or fifty. King Richard laughed and yelled that it was an ambush. The horses reared, the dogs yelped, and the French King was thrown from his horse. Oscar was busy controlling his horse and trying to watch where the falcon flew. Dubois was again nowhere to be seen.

Finally with a hard, "Ho!" King Richard decided he would take matters into his own hands, and he spurred on his heavy steed. He pulled out his broadsword and lay siege to the largest boar in the pack. The boar was also now bearing down on the defenseless and drenched king of France. Timmy rode behind the king and tried to follow as best he could. Richard screamed a battle cry catching up to the tusked monster of three hundred pounds. Now in a full gallop, Richard threw one leg over, stepped firmly on the saddle, and pushed off high into the air. King Richard with his sword over his head and the blade pointed down like a thunderbolt toward the large boar was a spectacal to behold. Timmy thought the sight was unmatched against anything he had ever seen, or for that matter would ever see again. When the king finally came down, the boar tried to change direction, probably sensing the human projectile coming straight for him, but it was too late. The king's sword connected and impaled the animal straight through the top of the neck and down a foot into the wet earth, bringing the creature to an abrupt stop a few feet from Phillip, who sat in the mud shaking.

Timmy got off his horse and went to help the king. "King Richard, my liege, are you all right?"

Richard got to his feet with a grand smile and spit the dirt out of his mouth. "We shall have meat, compliments of the king." They both laughed, and Richard put his arm around Timmy. Then he took his dagger, cut a six-inch tusk from the beast, and gave it to Timmy. "For you, dear Tim, in remembrance of this day." Timmy bowed, and the rest of the group moved in to help King Phillip. Richard offered his hand, and the wet king was pulled from the marsh. "Don't look so sad, cousin. You are safe and well."

Oscar now attended to his king. Dubois showed up minutes later with the falcon on his fist. Phillip looked at Dubois, then at Richard and if looks could kill ... He said, "Richard, the conqueror of Acre, Captain of the holy crusade, you seem to have yet another title: master of the marsh hog."

"Well, my royal drenched one, I will fill it with full humility and we will all enjoy this hog greatly at tonight's feast. Richard whispered to Dubois, "I should think you might appreciate my help in this matter. Not only did I do the falcon's job and put meat on the table for tonight's feast, but I saved your illustrious master and king. How is it that you were lost to the group?"

Timmy and Oscar started to laugh but stopped short as both kings frowned at them to be silent. Richard continued in a lighter tone. "Phillip, hunting is in its nature unpredictable, as you well know. Let us continue. We've ten falcons to fly, and daylight is getting short."

Phillip grimaced but agreed. "Let me get warm and dry, and we shall continue." The group took a badly needed break.

CHAPTER 5

"Wendover is it? This bird must die."
And… smelly cheese

AFTER THE MISHAP IN the marsh, the hunting party decided to go east and seek upland game. Things came together for Dubois, and two of his birds performed magnificently. As for Timmy, he was happy to see his hawks make a kill every time they were put on game. The dogs were flawless, and the Kings were royally amused. But Wendover's final flight was postponed, for the tour de force of the sun had to yield to the adventures of the moon. The feast could be smelled for miles as the hunting group and their growling tummies made their way back to camp. Everyone was tired and dirty but glowing from the day's events out in the field. Never could King Richard remember a better day of hunting. Even the French king was satisfied that there was something special about the day.

Sara met Timmy as the group reached camp. Sara was so proud of Timmy that she swelled up as he got closer.

"You, my lord, are the talk of the hunt. You helped King Richard kill that beast, and ..."

Timmy stopped her. "I'm very tired, and King Richard has summoned me straight away. Can we talk later?" Sara stood alone as Timmy walked past her. She was confused but dismissed Timmy's lack of enthusiasm for the day's events. "I'll see you at the feast, then," she said as he passed into the doorway of the mews.

He did not trust her now, and he did not know what to do. He couldn't tell Cornelius because he might take her away. He definitely could not speak to Connie or Stanley because they could not keep their mouths shut. He was at a loss. He would have to face her and ask her why she consorted with Oscar when peace was on the line between their countries. Then he pondered the unthinkable. What if she was in love with him? He began to torture himself with the idea, "So, *she likes the French falconer's assistant better than me. I can live with it. I will never love again, but I will get by in a world of kings and falcons...FALCON"* Then it occurred to him. He could talk to Wendover, he might know what to do.

Wendover was in his normal spot, and Timmy looked around the mews to assure himself that no one else was in the room. He leaned in toward Wendover. "It looks like tomorrow will be our last day together."

Wendover looked keenly at the boy, who was becoming a young man. "Every bird in your care flew with style and grace today. You should be proud." Timmy smiled but then frowned. "What's the matter?"

"It's Sara, Wendover. I saw her sneak out and meet with the French falconer's assistant, Oscar. They talked, and then at the end she kissed and hugged him. It was a long hug, too. Could she be a spy in love with a Frenchman, Wendover?"

Wendover cocked his head. "My expertise is not in the field of love or intrigue, my dear master. I am but a falcon on the king's perch. But I have seen you together—the way she smiles at you, how she acted when you had your first kiss. I would say there must be something in the wind that makes her court danger. She may even be in danger herself."

Timmy thought for a moment and decided he had been a fool. Sara was his girl, and he would do anything for her just as he would for king and country. *She must be in trouble,* he thought, and he knew he must ask her. "Thank you, Wendover. I will see you soon. I must go and find Sara."

He left the mews before Wendover could say, "Be careful." Wendover sat on the perch worried when who should appear out of the fresh oat hay but DJ. "Wendover, I heard every word. Is there anything I can do?"

Wendover thought for a while. Then he looked down at DJ and exclaimed, "I have an idea."

DJ listened as Wendover drew out a plan. Then with more speed than grace, the rat was on his way. He scampered out the mews through a guard's legs and toward the king of France's mews. He saw Oscar and Dubois huddled in the back, talking. The little pack rat extraordinaire quietly made his way around the French guards and finally found himself within earshot of the two. It was then he smelled the most wonderful aroma of cheese. He looked down to see Pierre la Dubois's lunch laid out for him. *The French make the best cheese in the world,* he thought.

DJ's cheese moment was interrupted by Dubois and his angry display of the day's events and he hid behind the hunk of smelly Roquefort. "If you would have done your job the way we'd planned, the king would have never been hurt."

Oscar looked down and seemed to take the insult in stride. Then Dubois took it one step too far and raised his hand to Oscar. Just when it looked as though he would be beaten, Oscar caught the old man's fist with his own, and lowered it calmly. "With all due respect, my master, it was no one's fault that the boars were in the marsh. No one could have known. As for you releasing a falcon on the pigs, it was only a human mistake. Anyone would have done the same."

Dubois, red faced and angry, pulled his fist from the lad and moved to his plate, where he took a knife and cut a huge chunk of cheese just inches from DJ, then he took some bread and stuffed the two in his mouth. He mumbled under his breath at least a half dozen words that were not understandable, but the intent was obvious. Oscar left the mews, and Dubois sat, fumed with anger, ate, and finished a bottle of wine.

DJ hunkered down and waited until Dubois moved away to look over an injured falcon. Then he stole a hunk of smelly cheese. *After all, pack rats need to eat, too,* he thought.

Another man came into the mews, and he wore a black and blood red cloak. His gloves were worn, and he had a large scar down his right cheek. It gave DJ the shivers. "The king has charged me with informing you that you have one last chance to complete the plan he has prescribed. The English king's favorite falcon, Wendover, is it? This bird must die, or you, my good master falconer, will lose all that is dear to you." Dubois started to stutter, and the man put his black gloved finger to Dubois's lips and said, "Let your words turn to deeds, monsieur. Less talk, old man, and more action." The caped man left Dubois in a cold sweat.

Dubois went over to the corner of the room and uncovered the cage of death. He peered at its sharp spikes, raised his goblet of wine and whispered, "Death to Wendover!"

DJ ran as fast as his little legs would carry him. He jumped, dodged, and leapt, curving around poles and climbing up logs to get to Wendover. But when he got to the mews, Wendover was gone. He did not know what to do, and so shouted at the other birds. He tried to talk with them, but none would reply. "Wendover is in trouble! Don't you see? Something terrible is afoot!"

In the main tent the last night's feast was under way, and the cooks and the servants busily worked for the largest event of the trip. The best wine and ale flowed for the kings and nobles. Barons and earls were invited to partake in the reverie, and everyone wanted to bend the kings' ear for favors. The French king would try to cajole the

English king's favorite vassals, and the English king would try to persuade the French king's barons to see his claim to French lands. All would be politics at their worst.

Timmy had gone to find Sara, and Sara had gone to find Oscar. Connie looked for Stanley, and DJ searched for Wendover. In such a small camp, it was amazing that no one could find the person he or she sought. Connie passed Timmy and asked him if he had seen Stanley. Connie looked down as he spoke to his friend, and Timmy could see that something was wrong. "What's wrong with my favorite mate, eh, Connie?"

Connie kicked the ground a bit, but finally came out with it. "I should ask *you*, Tim. You've been barking orders at Stanley and me like you was the king of England ... which you aren't, by the way."

Timmy saw that Connie's feelings were hurt, and he put his hand on his shoulder and apologized. "I'm sorry. It's just that things are so strange in this hunt, and ... Well, if you can keep a secret, I'll tell you what's really bothering me." Connie nodded his head. Timmy told him the story of Sara and Oscar. Connie said he would knock Oscar's block off. Timmy made Connie be quiet and still while he finished the rest of the story. "The main thing is that I think Wendover is in big trouble, and Sara too. I think the French king is going to try to pull something underhanded, but I don't know what it could be."

Connie listened, and when Timmy finished, he offered his advice. "Well, we shall have to keep an eye on Oscar and Dubois. You should talk to Sara. She is a good girl and if she is in danger we have to do something." The two finished and shook hands; they were friends again. Connie went off to find Stanley and tell him the story. Timmy went to find Sara.

Sara had found Stanley and asked him if he thought that Tim's feelings had changed for her. "Stanley, he walked right past me this afternoon with hardly a word. He acts like he hates me,"

Stanley tried to calm her down. "You are the air Timmy breathes, Sara. He has been short with us, too, barking orders at everyone. Something is definitely wrong." They parted with a hug, and Stanley went off to find Connie.

Finally, Timmy came back to the mews to find that Wendover was gone. Timmy panicked, and in a rage he went straight to the French falconer's tent to face Dubois. Timmy entered the tent, where Dubois was just finishing up the last of some wine and cheese. As soon as Timmy saw Dubois, he knew he had been rash, and all his accusations evaporated into the best thing he could think up to say at the moment. "I am looking for Oscar. Do you know where I might find him?" Timmy said as he flourished a bow.

"Young master, it would not be courteous of me to ignore your fine luck of flights. Though it seems that we as your guests have not enjoyed the same amount of success, I have only to wonder what you have been up to, my dear ambitious young falconer."

Timmy frowned but tried with all his might not to scream his outrage at the old man's statement. "You are without a doubt a very gifted master. I would say that falconers make their own luck with practice in the art of it."

"Foul play has been afoot, my dear laddy, and I will see that the king of France hears of it." Timmy was now red with anger and knew he should leave, but when he tried, Dubois stopped him. "You think I am a fool? I have been pulling these kinds of tricks since before you were born. I say that you will not get away with it."

"Let me pass, sir, or I will be forced to …"

As if the scene had been prepared by Shakespeare himself, Cornelius entered the tent as Timmy started to draw his sword. Cornelius broke in and said, "Tim my lad, here you are. Monsieur Dubois, I am sure that you two have been discussing the finer points of king's falconry, but alas, Timmy, the king has summoned you to his chambers before tonight's feast. I have only to tell you that it is a great honor that awaits you." Cornelius smiled at Dubois. Dubois sneered at Timmy, and Cornelius parted the way for Timmy's exit. "Now, off you go, lad." Timmy left the tent and waited outside for his father to conclude his business with Dubois.

Cornelius paused and walked around the tent. He turned and noticed the large covered object in the corner of the room. Then he smiled at Dubois. "Doesn't Tim remind you of someone? Think back to years ago."

Dubois stepped aside and slumped down in his chair. "These times have not been as easy for me as you, Cornelius. Your king loves his birds to fly high for the sake of the art, the chase, and the kill. My king would rather bet his royal underwear and drink himself into bed, not ever caring to see a falcon show its true majesty." Dubois looked about to see whether anyone had heard his confession.

Cornelius spoke in soft tones. "I am sorry, old friend, but do not test my king's resolve. He has been known to lift cheaters up with his sword rather than see them hang."

Dubois sobered and scoffed. "I will see you at the feast."

Cornelius left, and Timmy ambushed him outside. "Wendover is gone, and I know that poor excuse for a man has him. I just pray they have not hurt him."

Cornelius smiled and set his hand upon Timmy's shoulder. "Calm down, lad. You could have caused an international incident in there."

Timmy rushed on with resolve. "I will take my sword and ..."

At that moment Cornelius shook Timmy hard, and he looked at his master with eyes of disbelief. "Calm heads and steady hearts get the work done! Isn't that what you've learned, flying the king's falcons? It's the reason you have gone so far at such a young age in the world, your even temper and your brains." Cornelius put both hands on Timmy's shoulders now and changed his tone to a whisper. "I took Wendover, lad, for his own safety. Remember that it's your job to look after Wendover but it's my job to look after all of you. You are right, there is espionage in the air, and I am privy to it. Not the whole plan, but bits and pieces. I told you once, and I will now ask you again: let me handle the dirty work. You fly your birds and give a good show. I love you, lad, but you must do as I say."

Timmy bowed his head a bit and then looked up into Cornelius's sparkling green eyes to see the man's love. "I will, father. I will do my job. I am sorry for forgetting to use my head."

Cornelius hugged him. "There'll be time enough for you to use your sword in the king's name, but for now go get cleaned up for the feast." Timmy started off, and Cornelius shouted after him. "I'm proud of ya, lad. Very proud."

Timmy ran off with a soaring heart and a plan to fight for Sara, Wendover, and of course, the king.

CHAPTER 6

"Glory be...It's a world of Spies, intrigue
And mortal enemies"

THE MUSIC OF LIVELY lutes, drums, and recorders filled the air as all the guests gathered in the center of the camp. Barons and earls arrived and took their seats at the huge feasting table. The kings sat side by side and watched as Jugglers, fire breathers and the French court jester amused them. There must have been fifty people at the kings' table, wine and ale was poured with great delight. Timmy sat next to Sara, and Cornelius was on his other side, next to King Richard.

Sara whispered to Timmy, "What did you do with Wendover? We were all shocked to see he was not in the royal mews."

Timmy mustered a smile. "If you think that you were shocked, just think how I felt. I walked in, and he was gone you can't imagine the thoughts I had. But never fear—my father took charge of his safety."

Cornelius heard the whispers and added, "Wendover is happy and content in my tent, under guard. We look forward to a spectacular flight in the morning, and then he will belong to the king of France."

Sara looked at Timmy and saw him try to grin. "It's alright, Sara. If I am to lose my prize bird, it is good I do it in the name of peace and King Richard."

Richard faintly heard his name, and took account and stood tall to propose a toast. "I am not a humble king, but I wish everyone here well, for the hunting has been grand and the company unmatched in thine eyes. To my friend and cousin, the king of all France. May his birds fly high and his expectations be wide, and may our people be at peace for all the ages." The onlookers clapped, whistled, and made merry the occasion.

The feast was endless: smoked meats, moor hen, pheasant, and the wild boar that King Richard had killed. The head, minus one tusk, was in front of the king's plate with an apple in its mouth. As the evening wore on, noble birds of feather pulled together. It was the French barons fawning or demanding attention of the French King, and English earls sucking up to the English king. Several times the kings disagreed and insulted each other—only to embrace and apologize moments later. The more wine that was drunk, the more fighting that sprang up. It was time for the feast to be done, and the great kings stood as well as they could and announced the reverie over. Everyone started to move to their respective tents and fires. Cornelius watched as Dubois disappeared, and then he disappeared himself.

Oscar was waiting outside the camp. He had no fire and had been waiting for an hour. He was chilled to the bone, and his teeth chattered as a man moved toward him. He watched as he grew closer and started to pull his sword. It was not until the two were almost face to face that the man unhooded himself and spoke. It was Cornelius "what have you for me, Oscar?"

"My lord, 'tis the will of the king of France, and the master falconer's charge, to play havoc with the bird known as Wendover. Dubois has given me the task of spoiling the flight with means of a death cage, and also a backup plan of a sharp set goshawk that I hath purchased. It is my order to hide out into the wood and make death of the falcon by any means I can."

"Dubois has sunk, lad. He has fallen to the depths of the devil. What else do you know on the king's front?"

Oscar looked around and got even closer. "The king of France does not know of which I speak now—he is not part of *this* plan. The man with a crimson cape has a plot against King Richard. I listened in and was not seen, but they want King Richard dead, my lord. Of what means, I do not know, but I do know it is to happen on the last flight of the day."

Suddenly there was a rustle in the bushes, and both put their hands on their swords. Cornelius looked at the bush and walked toward it to get a closer look. DJ had been listening, and when he climbed up to see out, he had placed his paw on a nest of sparrows. The mother sparrow flew away in fright. "Nothing here," Cornelius spoke in calm tones. DJ took exception and rustled a few more bushes to make his point. The two went on with their conversation, and DJ listened intently.

"Go back and learn whatever else you can," and Cornelius once again put his hood over his head. "I'll meet you at dawn. No, on second thought I will send Sara. Oscar, take care of yourself. These people are dangerous."

Oscar looked at the old man in front of him and smiled. "Thank you, my lord."

"No, thank *you*, Oscar. You are a hero. Soon you and Sara will be together again."

Cornelius and Oscar went their separate ways and disappeared into the mist. DJ scampered just behind Cornelius and followed him back to his tent. As the two entered DJ saw Wendover was perched next to a small fire. Cornelius took no time to undress and wrap himself up in the covers of a good night's sleep.

DJ moved close to a hooded Wendover and with the soft tones of an Irish tenor squeaked in his familiar voice. "Wendover, I have arrived. I have found ya!"

Wendover replied, "I did not know I was lost. DJ, please remove my hood so that I can see where I am."

DJ did as requested, and the hood tumbled down off the falcon. The rat told him his story, "Wendover, they are going to try to kill ya. Oh yes, and the king, too. These people are bad, Wendover, real bad, and there is more. Oscar and Sara are not just friends, but they will be together soon, and poor Timmy will have his heart broken in two. Glory be! It's a world of spies, intrigue and mortal enemies."

Wendover was trying to take it all in, but DJ was going too fast. "DJ, please slow down. Now, who is trying to kill whom?"

"The king of France wants you dead."

But why would he want me dead if he is going to get me as a gift?"

DJ pondered on that. "I don't know, but there is more. Our king is also in danger. There is a plot on his life, and it will all happen on the last flight of the day."

Wendover cocked his head and thought for a second. "What about Sara?"

"She and Oscar will soon be together again. I heard Cornelius speak of it."

Wendover hung his head. DJ waited for a response, but it never came. The two did not know what to do.

In the morning there was the hustle and bustle of horses, falcons, and servants, the last day of the hunt was upon them. Timmy could not find Sara, and Oscar had disappeared, too. Timmy started thinking that Sara may be in danger, but he had falcons to ready for the kings' hunt, and he trusted that Cornelius was doing his job.

Wendover was finally returned to Timmy. Cornelius brought him in and set him down on the perch. "You'd better check that hood. Wendover threw if off last night."

Timmy smiled at the falcon and could not contain his happiness at seeing the bird. "Wendover, you are safe!"

Cornelius smiled, too. "Well, let us make this a day to remember, eh, lads?"

The three chummed up and bellowed a healthy "Aye, for king and country."

Cornelius moved outside and started barking orders. Wendover and Timmy stared at each other, and Wendover started to speak. "It seems that I am in danger."

Timmy frowned. "How do you know that?"

"Also, more important is that the king is in danger as well." Timmy stared in disbelief at what he was hearing. "I don't know how to tell you this but... Sara and Oscar are ..."

Timmy broke in. "Yes, I know, but Cornelius is aware of all the plots and he said we must concentrate on our part. Our job Wendover, is to fly high and be ready for anything" With that he checked his broadsword and reached for its grip. Wendover looked at his master. "Fly high and fly fast." Timmy grinned as he climbed up into the saddle of the massive stallion.

Soon the hunting processional was in place and waited for the two kings to mount their horses. Still Timmy looked for Oscar and Sara, but they were nowhere to be seen. The man with the crimson cape was also missing. Timmy started to worry that something terrible had happened to one of the kings, but just as he was going to ask Cornelius, King Richard came out with a blanket around him. The announcement came from the booming voice of the king himself. "The king is well and ready for the hunt." However, he did not look well: he shook and was almost as pale as the white horse he rode. The French king mounted as well, and the caravan was off.

The train sported falcons, dogs, wagons, and everything that composed a small moving town. There was intrigue in the air. The two kings rode side by side, and Cornelius and Dubois were behind them. There was always the complement of French and English knights in front and in back of the kings; they were heavily armed and ready for anything. Timmy thought that it would be impossible to try and kill King Richard.

As they rode, Oscar joined the group next to Timmy, he looked tired and beaten down. "You look like you have not slept in days," Timmy remarked.

Oscar smiled. "I have not—you are right. The French king has not been happy with the performance of his falcons or his falconers, and he has been making us pay dearly for it."

Timmy could not help himself and blurted out, "And maybe if you spent more time with your falcons and less time with Sara, you might be more successful."

Oscar stared at Timmy and gave him a look that would have meant sword play, had both their jobs not interfered. "What do you know about Sara and me?"

Timmy replied, "Well, let's see. I know that you have been seeing her outside the camp, and that she has not told me anything about that. I just happen to be her boyfriend, if you have not noticed."

Oscar quipped back, "You should not presume to my business, little lad."

That was the last straw. Timmy jumped off his horse and slammed into Oscar, knocking them both to the ground. The line stopped. Timmy drew his sword, as did Oscar. Oscar beckoned him. "Come on, little stump, let's see what you are made of."

Timmy let his sword fly to a cross cut, but Oscar blocked it easily. Timmy then thrust, and another block from Oscar's blade sent him off balance and into a bush. It was clear that Timmy was out of his element. Just when Oscar started to charge him, Sara rode up, got off her horse, and stood in between them. "What in the king's name are you two idiots doing? Trying to start a war?" They looked at her, and by now the two kings were also riding up to the fight.

King Richard shook as he spoke. "Does not this hunt interest you lads? You must fight instead? Furthermore, have you not heard that our countries are at peace? It is my command!"

Not to be outdone, Phillip added, "Oui, peace. Dubois, get your apprentice under control, or I shall ..." He stopped short, looked at Richard, and rode back to his place in line.

Richard said, "And you, my dear Tim. Place your energy upon the task of flying my falcons, or you will find yourself a full-time soldier, and that would be a waste of good falconry talent, would it not?"

Cornelius chimed in. "My apologies, Your Majesty. All will be well."

With that resolved, the king returned to his position, and Timmy and Oscar remounted their steeds. "This is not done," Oscar whispered under his breath; it was just audible to Timmy. Sara got back on her mare and rode to the back of the line. Timmy wanted to follow her but knew he had been put in his place, and he could not venture anywhere until all things were calm again.

Dubois and the man in the crimson cape were now riding together and they were starting to wonder why that girl and Oscar seemed to have looks between them that were all too familiar. It took very little to topple the best-laid plan, and they knew that spies came in all shapes, sizes, and sexes. "Dubois, you make sure you watch her and the lad. Something seems amiss."

Dubois grinned showing his toothless gap as he spurred his horse and headed for the back of the line, pretending to look after his falcons.

DJ had snuck underneath the cadge and found a place next to Wendover. He fed him as much information as he could while bouncing up and down as they were carried by two attendants. Every once in a while, one of the footboys would see him and try to kick at him and squish him. "Timmy and Oscar got into a fight, Wendover. It came to swords." Aye, and I'm afraid Timmy is not as adept at sword play as Oscar. I've seen Oscar practice, and he is very good!" DJ hung from the bottom of the carrier, and he flipped up and sat on the perch. "Well, Wendover, we know that someone is going to try and kill you today, and the king, too, but we don't know how or why."

At that point Oscar came riding back toward the falcons. DJ sneered. "There he is, Wendover, Oscar, your mortal enemy. He looks mean, too." At that point DJ had a courageous idea. He thought he could save the day. He whispered to Wendover, "I will go with Oscar and report back as soon as I can."

Wendover tried to rush a response, "It's too dangerous my friend," but DJ had already jumped on Oscar's horse and into one of his saddle bags. It just so happened that it was the one containing Oscar's lunch.

"Aye tis gooey cheese. Mm, good," the rat said.

CHAPTER 7

"Nasty deeds will take place this day"

THE LARGE HUNTING GROUP had ridden for almost three hours, the weather was perfect and it looked like they had reached the best hunting grounds yet. Deer played in the countryside, wild boar and red squirrels were plentiful. Moor fowl and pheasant abounded. At the kings' decree, the camp was set. King Richard looked like he felt better and was free of the shakes that had plagued him. Timmy, Stanley, and Connie were busy getting the birds in flying order, and the stage was set for the French king's falcons to start the day.

Pierre la Dubois had picked a wonderful flying peregrine for his first flight. Her name was Diana, and she was attended to just like the goddess of the hunt that was her namesake. This time pointing dogs had been released to find moor fowl. It was not long before the French Spaniels struck their customary pose, tail straight up in the air. The chase was about to begin.

The king was handed the bird, and let it loose. The longwing rang up into the blue sky. The king watched as Dubois and Oscar kicked around the thicket to flush the bird, and flush it did. The red hen flew low to the ground as fast as an arrow. Diana saw it flush and stooped down as if she had done the deed a thousand times. She hit the bird straight in the head, and the feathers sprinkled the air as it fell to the ground. The crowd cheered.

The day wore on, and many flights were successful. The oohs and aahs of the onlookers filled the English countryside. Richard was not feeling himself, though, and finally called for a mid-day nap. After a rest he would be ready for the highlight of the day. Wendover versus a pheasant. He was off to his tent with sleepy eyes. The pause, gave King Richard and Wendover's enemies time to position themselves in the proper place. The man in the crimson cape set out his men for the attack and Cornelius countered with the king's defenses, which he checked and rechecked.

The caped man now changed into a disguise. He covered his face in mud, and put on a dirty old jerkin and hat. His next task was to draw back his weapon, the most lethal one of its time, he put his foot in the stirrup and pulled back the lath and string of the crossbow. The final act was to place the sharp quarrel laced with hemlock onto the catch of the crossbow. He hid it underneath a drab green cloak, smiled to himself and left the tent. Dubois looked for Oscar but couldn't find him and was finally made to prepare the cage of death himself. Meanwhile, Oscar followed the man with the scar as the assassin got in line for a good shot at King Richard.

Timmy held Wendover and spoke to him in soft tones. "My best friend, you are in danger today. You must only focus on the prey I flush for you. Let this be our best fight together."

Wendover scratched at his hood a little, and Timmy heard his comments. "I shall master Tim, this will be the flight of my life. I will miss you, you have been much more than my master—you are my friend and teacher."

Timmy replied, "No, Wendover, it is you who has been the teacher. I would have never dreamed possible the things we have done."

With that Sara moved close beside Tim and took his arm. "Timmy, I think it's time you should know something about me and ..."

Timmy filled in the blank. "Oscar?" Sara smiled, looked at the ground, and fidgeted a little. Finally Timmy blurted it out. "I know you are in love with him. I hope you two will be very ..." He could not keep a tear from falling down his cheek.

Sara took her finger and caught the droplet, looking dismayed and confused. "Yes, I *do* love Oscar—but not in the way you think. Timmy, you poor lad, he's my brother."

"What? He's your brother, as in kin? As in you probably won't be marrying him?"

Sara laughed. "No, Timmy, I promise I will not be marrying my brother."

"Wendover, did you hear that? She won't be …"

Sara shushed him and covered his mouth with her hand. She whispered, "Tim, Oscar is a spy, for our king, and you must not speak of this thing out loud. This is very serious. Do you understand?" Timmy nodded, and she pulled her hand from his mouth and replaced it with the most intense kiss he had ever experienced. All Connie and Stanley could do was sigh as they watched.

The trumpets finally rose up their fanfare at the sight of King Richard returning to the hunt. However, to Timmy they might as well have been wedding bells, because he was in a world all his own. Cornelius bumped him out of his moment of love, he looked at Sara, smiled, and was off towards the King's side. Cornelius asked Sara what had gotten into Tim, and she smiled and giggled. He decided to leave young love well enough alone and went on about his business.

King Richard and the French king were twenty feet apart on wooden thrones, and the French king had his feet up and was sipping a goblet of fine wine. Richard had a strong ale to help calm his fever. The time had come for Wendover's last flight. King Richard stood up and seemed to gain strength with the action, he looked at Timmy holding the little prince of a falcon, then faced Phillip. He spoke with a serious tone "That our two countries may live in peace, Phillip, may I dedicate this flight to you, and after, make a gift of this superb falcon, Wendover." Phillip choked on his wine then stood and hugged the English King. At the same time he was looking for Dubois or anyone to call off the cage of death, but to no avail. Richard, Timmy and Wendover, were upon their steeds and out in the field before he could change the tide of events. King Phillip started to sweat. Dubois was busy with the cage of death, ready to lure Wendover to his doom. A very wild pheasant was placed in the cage and started to jump up and down trying to fly. Dubois believed Wendover would not be able to resist and come down and impale himself.

If King Richard were to know all the plots the day sported, he would have felt exhilarated to learn that even when he was at play, battles were taking place in his name right under his nose.

As Timmy and the lads searched for the scent of a pheasant, the words hung in their minds. "Nasty deeds will take place this day."

DJ, unbeknownst to Oscar had hidden in his hawking bag as he followed the man with the scar and held the gold hair pin like a little sword and was ready to use it as a weapon. He crept to where the man with the crossbow was silently waiting for his moment, and stood inches from the man's boot. Oscar was in place, with the very sharp set goshawk that he intended to let loose on the villain. It seemed everyone was set for the play to begin, and Wendover's hood was the curtain.

Timmy surveyed the crowd, the kings, the dog—all the things seemed to go in slow motion. The king struck the braces of the hood, and a wild pheasant flushed prematurely as Wendover roused. The king thought that maybe Wendover would try to tail chase the bird and thus the flight would be ruined, but Wendover stood as still as a prayer, cocked his head at Timmy then blasted off from the king's fist so fast that all who watched were in awe of the small bird's speed. The king smiled at Timmy and he bowed his head for his Monarch. Up and up Wendover went, looking down on the whole world. "Now this is what I'm talking about," he roused again in midflight as he continued climbing. Then as all smart falcons do, he surveyed the English countryside for eagles or other birds of prey that may be a danger to him.

The king of France quipped to Richard, "He will fly so high that he will disappear into heaven, and the flight will be over." His entourage laughed and watched the little bird go higher and higher till he was just a spot.

Wendover now waited on for Timmy's command, but as he waited, he saw the whole world of danger unfolding before him. Dubois was next to the cage of death. The man with the crossbow stood still, and twenty paces off, Oscar held a goshawk ready to pounce on the caped man. Then Wendover saw something that made him worry. Twelve men were closing slowly on the kings, and they had their swords out and looked like they would be attacking King Richard. But then he also saw men dressed in green on the tops of the trees, with bows and arrows at the ready.

Down on the ground Timmy twirled his gauntlet, which was Wendover's sign to get ready to dive. Timmy's words rang true in the falcon's mind: "Let this be our best flight together."

Down on the ground, Timmy directed Connie and Stanley to flush the pheasant, and both lads whooped and hollered. Bella pounced. And Timmy burst forth with his call "Wing over Wendover!!!" It was magnificent: the large rooster pheasant flushed, its wings beating hard and fast and its primordial squawk rang everyone's ears as it rose up like a battle cry. Up, high it went, and it never stopped climbing. Wendover cocked his head, folded his body inward, and stooped at the prey. Timmy looked up, and as he did, he caught a movement in his right eye. He turned to look and saw a man with a crossbow aiming at the king, but then he saw a small pack rat piercing the man's foot with a hat pin. Then he saw Oscar loosing the goshawk at the caped man. Timmy looked to his left and saw men with swords running at the king. He pulled his sword, but just as the men started to close in, other men came screaming out of the forest; they were all dressed in green and shot arrows true to their mark, stopping the attacking men in their tracks. Oscar ran to the caped man and pulled his goshawk off him, but not before he'd bashed the man with the round part of his broad sword. The man wasn't too hurt, but the bird had grabbed him by the head and left a nasty cut and talon marks. There was also a small hole in his boot. DJ sat on a bramble and thrust the gold pin high in the air, making his victory yell, which was more squeak and less shout. "Glory be! God save the King!"

Sara ran toward Timmy and as he turned to embrace her he tripped and fell to the ground, hitting his head on a round large rock all the lights went out. The last thing he said was,

"Sara"... then..." Where is Wendover?"

EPILOGUE

"Isn't this great, being a part of a dream?"

WHEN TIMMY AWOKE, IT was to very wet kisses. He lay in the grass whispering Sara's name, then Wendover's. Finally when his eyes opened to the world, he said, "Oh Roxy, stop, will ya?" Roxy got one more lick in for luck, and Timmy sat up just in time to see Wendover smash the pheasant. His first instinct was to rush to Wendover's side, but as he rose he found he was dizzy. Then it all came back to him in one big rush of memory, vivid and true. He could smell the roast meat and feel the crisp English air in his nostrils. King Richard was his king and master, wasn't he? He remembered Cornelius, his father. Pictures of Connie and Stanley and him wrestling in the wet hay, and then the long perch filled with falcons that were his charge. Then there was the plot to kill Wendover.

His mind stopped dead in its tracks. *Sara!* He touched his lips. Then looked down to feel his broad sword, but it no longer was there. "Oh my, Roxy. Methinks that I am not in England anymore." He walked to Wendover and the dead pheasant. Roxy ran circles around him, he felt for the lump on his head and reached for the golden pheasant feather that had adorned his hat, but found his baseball cap instead. He looked around for Wendover.

"Wendover! Am I glad to see you. Hey, boy, that was a one heck of a flight, are you alright?" But Timmy received no reply in his head. He thought for a moment and shook his head a little. "Oh, I think I get it. Boy that was one heck of a dream. Wendover, I dreamed that we could talk to each other like people do ... Well, not like people, but in our minds. We ..."

Just then Wendover looked up at Timmy, roused, cocked his head and winked. For a moment Timmy was dumbfounded, but then a big smile came upon his face. Wendover looked back at the pheasant and Timmy looked down at Wendover and the two thought to themselves, *isn't this great, being a part of a dream?*

The End

ABOUT THE AUTHOR

Eric Stephen Bocks lives in Le Grand, California, and spends his time farming almonds, composing music, writing books, and of course flying birds of prey at worthy quarry. At the time of this writing, hunting season is in full swing, and the California drought is taking a small break while clouds pour four to eight inches of rain throughout its parched lands. Wendover is in great shape even though he was injured at the end of last hunting season. Roxy is limping a little but is solid in her hunting. Bella, the English setter, is pointing pheasants, and Tess, the black Lab, is the new addition to the hunting team and is learning her way around ducks and other game birds. Eric is pleased to share *Wendover Meets the King* and is excited about the coming year of book signings, as well as promoting all the other books in this unique falconry series. *Wendover meets the King* also has a unique place in Eric's heart, as it includes the character King Richard the lion heart. Eric has also written, composed and starred in the off Broadway hit musical *Heart of the lion*. The musical boasts a different story of the King, including Robin Hood and a cast of his merry men and evil villains. As always, Eric hopes to keep writing Wendover's adventures for years to come, and he endeavors to bring the art of falconry closer to his readers while always being truthful and respectful of this ancient art.

ABOUT THE BOOK

Wendover Meets the King is the third book in the Wing over Wendover series from author Eric Stephen Bocks. Wendover is a peregrine falcon that hunts at the pleasure of his sixteen-year-old master falconer, Timmy. Wendover is joined in his adventures by Diego Maximillian Jones, a small but very passionate pack rat who helps him and Timmy in all their exploits.

In *Wendover Meets the King,* our team takes on a new spirit of falconry. The story starts with Timmy watching Wendover fly high in the sky. While flushing a pheasant, Timmy looks up, trips, and bumps his head at the moment Wendover power dives toward the game bird. All the lights go out for Timmy.

When Timmy awakes, he finds himself in a strange land, but it's not just the land that is peculiar—time has changed, too. He is now eight hundred years in the past, in Medieval England and at the court of King Richard the Lionheart. He learns that his role in this kingdom is as the king's master falconer, in charge of flying sixteen of the king's best hunting falcons. Timmy is thrust into a world of intrigue, and there is soon to be a great hunt. King Phillip of France and King Richard will fly their falcons, drink wine, and talk politics.

But all is not so grand. The French king's falconer, Dubois, is an evil man and wants to harm Wendover. Also a mysterious man with a scar dressed in a red cloak has a dangerous surprise for King Richard. *Wendover Meets the King* is full of fun, danger, and even a little romance, as Timmy meets a girl who is a friend and tries to combine those two words into one: girlfriend. Wendover flies high, DJ plots, and they all try to save the king. Huzzah! God save the king!

GLOSSARY OF TERMS

BRACES-THIN STRIPS OF LEATHER TO PULL TIGHTEN A HOOD

BRANCHER-YOUNG HAWK JUST ABOUT TO FLY FROM NEST

CADGE- A MOVABLE PERCH FOR TRAVELING WITH FALCONS

CERE- SOFT PART ON EITHER SIDE OF A BIRDS BEAK

COCKERAL-SIX WEEK OLD CHICKEN

FLUSH- TO MAKE PREY MOVE SO THAT A FALCONER CAN CATCH IT

GAUNTLET-GLOVE USED IN FALCONRY TO CARRY BIRDS OF PREY

GOBLET-CUP

GOSHAWK-SHORT WINGED HAWK

HEMLOCK-POISEN FROM A HEMLOCK TREE

HERON- LARGE BIRD THAT LIVES IN THE MARSHES

"HO HO HO"-A WAY OF CALLING ATTENTION
   TO PREY TO THE FALCON

HOOD-SOFT IMPLEMENT TO COVER A
   FALCON'S HEAD

HOME CROFT- FARM

HUZZAH-WORD OF CELEBRATION OR
   AKNOWLEDGMENT

JERKIN-VEST

MATE- FRIEND

MEWS-A KEPT BIRD OF PREYS HOME

MOORHEN-RED GROUSE

PERCH-PLACE WHERE A BIRD SITS

PIKE- LONG SPEAR

PREY-THE HUNTED

RAPTOR-BIRD OF PREY

ROQUEFORT-TYPE OF BLUE CHEESE

ROUSE-TO SHAKE WITH CONTENTMENT

SLIP-FALCONRY TERM MEANING TO HUNT A
   FALCON ON PREY

TAIL CHASE-BIRD OF PREY CHASES PREY
   WITHOUT PITCH

TALON-CLAW OF A BIRD OF PREY

VASSAL-LAND OWNER LOYAL TO A KING OR
   QUEEN

COMING SOON

WINGOVER WENDOVER

AND

DJ'S ANCESTRAL TREASURE

FOR DETAILS ON
COMING EVENTS GO TO

WINGOVER WENDOVER.COM
ERIC STEPHEN BOCKS .COM

HAVE YOU READ THE OTHER BOOKS IN THE SERIES

WINGOVER WENDOVER

In the small town of Le grand California lived a boy and his falcon. Timmy was just 16 years old and could finally drive and drive he did…all those country roads he loved so much, hunting and flying his falcon. Being in the countryside, air as clean as the fresh wet grass and teeming with wild things that lived in every square inch of it, all he had to do was look

WINGOVER WENDOVER
LOST IN THE CITY

Wingover Wendover was definitely going on a trip. Diego Maximillian Jones —his trusty side kick and all around best friend and packrat fretted as he saw all kinds of different- looking cars and trucks. The landscape had changed from orchards and cattle land to tall skyscrapers. "The houses are huge! Giants must live here! They take up the whole sky"

Printed in the United States
By Bookmasters